The
Wishing
Tree

by RUTH CHEW

Illustrated by the author

SCHOLASTIC INC.
New York Toronto London Auckland Sydney

ISBN 0-590-30888-2

12 11 10 9 8 7 6   2 3 4 5/9

Printed in the U.S.A.   40 *for*

Emily Book Gloekler

"Peg, listen! There's that bird again! I wonder where he is. He sounds so close." Brian turned around and ran back into the park.

"Come back," Peggy called. "It's time to go home."

Their mother always said, "Prospect Park is not safe after dark." Peggy looked at the sky. It was beginning to turn pink.

Brian was running down the old stone walk. Peggy was older than her brother. She knew she had to make him leave the park. She raced after him.

The crumbling walk curved between the trees. Peggy was out of breath when she reached Brian. He was standing in the middle of the walk staring up into an old beech tree.

Brian pointed at the top of the tree. "There he is!"

Peggy looked up. The branches of the tree were bare. She could see the bird against the sky. It was November. But the bird had his head tipped back and was singing as if it were April.

He was about as big as a robin, but he was gray in color. At first Peggy thought he sounded like a robin. But then he changed his tune. He chirped and trilled and twittered a number of different songs.

The bird caught sight of the children. He cocked his head to look down at them. But he went on singing. He seemed to be happy to have someone listening to him. He sang and sang.

At last the bird stopped singing. He shook his feathers. Then he fluttered off the branch and flew up into the air and away.

Brian grabbed Peggy's arm. "Look at the tree," he whispered.

Peggy stared at the trunk of the tree. There seemed to be little faces peeking out of it.

"Peg, I'm scared!" Brian tugged at her arm.

"Don't be silly." Peggy pulled him over to the tree. As they came closer, they saw that the thick trunk was twisted and lumpy. "It's just the shadows on these lumps." Peggy reached out to touch the tree.

"Be careful how you fool with that tree!" someone said.

Peggy and Brian jumped back. They saw an old woman in a shabby brown coat and a floppy hat sitting on a stone bench beside the walk. Peggy and Brian had often seen her in the park. But she had never spoken to them.

"What did you say?" Peggy asked.

The woman was looking into the air where the bird had flown. She didn't answer when Peggy spoke to her. A shopping bag was lying on its side at her feet.

Brian pointed to the shopping bag. Peggy saw two shining eyes looking out of it. The next minute a striped gray cat slipped out and ran behind the tree.

"Your cat got away," Brian said.

The woman turned to look at him. She saw that the shopping bag was on its side, so she set it upright. Then she reached into it and took out a folded blue cloth. She gave the cloth a little pat and put it back into the bag.

The woman stood up. She picked up
the shopping bag and went down the
walk farther into the park. Peggy and
Brian walked the other way to get to
the park gate.

Peggy looked back at the tree. The
little faces on the twisted trunk
seemed to be laughing at her.

It was dark in the park now. The dry leaves on the walk made a whispery noise as the wind blew them along.

"It's spooky in here." Brian began to run. Peggy chased after him.

They didn't stop running until they had gone through the park gate and were on the sidewalk outside the tall iron fence.

"I know it's silly," Peggy said, "but I feel as if something is following us."

"Something is." Brian pointed. "Look!"

A striped gray tomcat was coming through the park gate. When he saw the children he sat down and watched them. But when they began to walk he got up and trotted along behind.

Peggy and Brian crossed the wide Brooklyn street by the park. They had to walk two blocks to the house where they lived. The cat followed them. They came to a corner and had to wait for a traffic light to change. The cat sat down and waited too.

When they reached home, Peggy rang the doorbell. Her mother opened the door.

"You're late," Mrs. Dobson said. "I was beginning to worry. Supper's almost ready."

Peggy walked into the house. Brian came in after her. And the gray cat slipped through the door after Brian.

"Who's this?" Mrs. Dobson asked.

The cat sat down in the middle of the front hall and looked up at her with big green eyes.

"He followed us home from the park, Mom," Brian said.

"He belongs to an old lady who spends a lot of time in the park," Peggy told her mother. "She keeps him in a shopping bag."

"He ran away from her." Brian walked over to the cat. "Didn't you, Puss?"

The cat rubbed against Brian's knee. Brian bent over to stroke him. The cat stood on his hind legs and reached up to pat Brian's cheek. He purred into his ear.

"Tomorrow's Saturday," Mrs. Dobson said. "You can take the cat back to the park and give him to the lady."

"She didn't seem to mind that he ran away," Peggy said.

"You still ought to give him back to her," Mrs. Dobson said. "Meantime,

I'll take him into the kitchen. Now go and get ready for supper."

Peggy and Brian hung up their jackets and went upstairs to wash their hands.

"Peg," Brian whispered. "That's no ordinary cat. We've got to get Mom to let us keep him."

"He looks about as ordinary as a cat can be." Peggy picked up the soap and started to lather her hands.

"Don't laugh, Peg. And promise you won't tell anybody." Brian took the soap from her.

"What are you trying to say?" Peggy rinsed her hands and dried them.

"That cat can talk!" Brian told her. "I called him *Puss*, and he said, 'How did you know my name?'"

"Peggy! Brian!" Mrs. Dobson was calling from the bottom of the stairs. "Hurry! Supper's on the table."

Peggy left the bathroom and went downstairs. Brian finished washing his hands and followed her. When they came into the dining room their father was already cutting up the pot roast.

Mrs. Dobson was serving it. "Pass me your plate, Peggy," she said.

Brian sat down at the table. "Mom, why don't we keep the cat?"

"He belongs to someone else, Brian," Mrs. Dobson said.

"Besides," Mr. Dobson added, "if you really want a cat, we should buy a kitten from a pet shop."

"The lady with the shopping bag

doesn't want Puss," Brian said. "You can come to the park with us tomorrow, Dad, and ask her yourself."

"What a good idea, George!" Mrs. Dobson said. "Why don't you go for a walk with the children? The exercise would do you good."

"The Army-Navy game is on television tomorrow." Mr. Dobson put down the carving knife and picked up his fork. "Would you please pass the potatoes."

"But, Dad," Brian said. "What about Puss?"

"I don't want to hear anything more about cats," Mr. Dobson said.

Peggy thought she'd better change the subject. "We heard a bird in the park, Daddy. It was all by itself in a tree. But it sang so many songs that it sounded as if the tree was full of birds."

"Now that is something worth talking about." Mr. Dobson put down his fork. "What color was the bird?"

"Gray," Brian told him.

"With a white patch on its wings," Peggy said. "I saw the white when it flew away."

"How big was it?" Mrs. Dobson asked.

"About like this." Brian showed her with his hands.

"It must have been a mockingbird," Mr. Dobson said. "I've read that some of them have come north. I haven't seen one since I was a kid in Virginia. There were lots there. My mother used to feed them."

Mrs. Dobson smiled. "Maybe this one will come to our bird feeder."

"Not if you keep a cat," Mr. Dobson said. "But anyway, they don't eat birdseed. My mother used to chop up raisins and fat for them."

When it was time for dessert, Mrs. Dobson took what was left of the pot roast into the kitchen. Peggy carried out the dinner plates.

The gray cat was sitting beside the garbage can. Mrs. Dobson took the plates from Peggy and scraped the leftover bits of fat and gravy into a pie pan. Then, to Peggy's surprise, her mother chopped off a hunk of meat from the pot roast and put it into the pan with the scraps. She put the pan on the floor beside the cat. "There you are, Puss."

The cat's green eyes opened wide. And so did his mouth. For a moment he looked as if he were going to say something. But Peggy knew cats can't talk. He just looked at Mrs. Dobson and then began to eat.

After supper everybody helped load the dishwasher. Then Peggy and Brian went to their rooms to do their homework. Mr. and Mrs. Dobson settled down in front of the television set in the living room.

Peggy copied over the words she'd had wrong in the spelling test in school. She read a chapter of her social studies book. Just as she was about to start her math, the bedroom door opened. Brian came in.

"I finished all my homework," he

said. "And I went to have a talk with Puss. But he won't have anything to do with me. He's watching television with Mom and Dad."

Peggy closed her math book. She had all the rest of the weekend to finish her homework. "Come on, Brian."

Mr. and Mrs. Dobson had been watching a program about exploring the bottom of the sea. The cat was sitting on the carpet staring at the television set. The end of his striped tail twitched whenever a fish swam across the screen.

Peggy and Brian came into the room just before the program ended. When it was over, Mr. Dobson turned off the set and picked up his newspaper. He made himself comfortable in his big easy chair and started to read.

Mrs. Dobson went to the kitchen to unload the dishwasher.

Brian and Peggy saw the cat get up and walk to the television set. He reached up a paw to push the switch that turned on the set.

An instant later, a young man playing a set of drums flashed onto the screen. The room was filled with the crash of loud music.

The cat ran under the sofa.

Mr. Dobson put down his newspaper. He got out of his chair and turned off the television. "Who turned that on?"

"Puss did," Brian blurted out.

His father looked at him. "I suppose you think that's funny, Brian. You know you're supposed to ask permission if you want to watch a program."

Peggy didn't like to see Brian blamed for something he hadn't done. "But, Daddy," she said, "the cat *did* turn on the set."

"That settles it," Mr. Dobson said. "It's off to bed for you two."

"I'm not sure I want to keep that cat after all," Brian told Peggy next morning after breakfast. "Do you think Dad really would let us have a kitten?"

"Don't believe it. He just wants you to get rid of me."

It didn't sound like Peggy's voice, but Brian couldn't see anyone else in the room. He looked at his sister. "Daddy wouldn't think of getting rid of you, Peg. I think he likes you more than he does me."

Peggy laughed. "I didn't say anything." She pointed to the floor.

The cat was right at her feet.

Brian stooped down. "You know you got us into trouble last night, Puss."

"I was just trying to get another look at those fish," the cat said. "How was I to know that awful noise would come out of the magic box. It was nice and quiet when the fish were swimming around in it. I'm sorry you were punished for what I did. But if I told your father the truth, he'd have thought he was going crazy. Grown-ups are like that."

"I've noticed," Brian agreed. "Sometimes I think you can't tell them anything."

Mrs. Dobson came into the room. The cat ran over to her and rubbed against her legs. She bent over and stroked his head. He purred loudly.

"Put on warm clothes, children. You have to take Puss back to his owner.

I'll give him something to eat while you're getting ready." Mrs. Dobson walked into the kitchen. The cat followed her.

Peggy and Brian went to get their jackets and hats and mittens.

When Mrs. Dobson came out of the kitchen, she was holding the cat in her arms. She handed him to Peggy. "Now remember, if you don't find the lady Puss belongs to, bring him back. Don't leave him in the park."

Mr. Dobson came downstairs. "That's right," he said. "It wouldn't be fair to the birds."

Brian and Peggy left the house by the front door. They started to walk to the park.

"You don't have to carry me," the cat said. "I can walk quite well by myself."

Peggy held onto the cat. "Mother

told me to give you to the lady with the shopping bag."

"Have it your way." The cat rested his front paws on Peggy's shoulder and enjoyed the ride.

They crossed the wide street and went in through the gate of the park. The sky was gray, and it was beginning to drizzle. There didn't seem to be anyone else in the park.

"I hate rain," the cat said. "It's a pity you didn't bring an umbrella."

Brian ran ahead down the stone walk. Peggy came after him, carrying the heavy cat. When they came close to the twisted old beech tree, they saw that the woman with the shopping bag was sitting on the bench where she had been yesterday.

She had spread a blue tablecloth on the walk. A bird was walking about on the cloth pecking at something. The woman was watching the bird. She didn't see the children.

Brian stopped walking. Peggy caught up to him. "Peg," he whispered. "Isn't that the mockingbird?"

Peggy stood quite still and looked at the woman. Her shopping bag was on the walk beside her. The woman had no umbrella. Her brown coat and floppy hat were getting wet. And her cheeks were pink with the cold. But she didn't seem to notice. She was too busy watching the bird eat.

The bird caught sight of Brian and Peggy and the cat. He flew up into the branches of the beech tree.

The woman looked up. As soon as she saw the children, she folded up the blue tablecloth and stuffed it into her shopping bag. She picked up the bag and jumped to her feet. Then she began to walk deeper into the park.

"Come back," Brian called. "Don't you want your cat?"

At this the woman started to run.

Peggy looked after her. "She seems to be afraid of something."

The rain was coming down harder now. "We'd better go home, Peg," Brian said.

Peggy's arms were tired. "Hold Puss for a minute."

Brian reached out to take the cat. Before he got hold of him, Puss jumped to the ground and ran over to the beech tree.

Both children rushed after him. When they came close to the tree they couldn't see the cat anywhere.

Peggy leaned on the tree. "We'd better find him," she said. "Mother told us not to leave him in the park."

Brian walked all around the tree. He couldn't find the cat. He looked up into the branches. The mockingbird was perched on one of them. He cocked his head and leaned over to get a better look at the children. Then he chirped something.

"I think you're trying to tell us something," Brian said.

The bird chirped again.

"I wish we could understand you," Peggy said.

The mockingbird hopped along the branch until he was right over Peggy's head. He opened his beak. But instead of chirping, he said, "Why don't you look inside the tree? That cat hates to get wet."

Peggy moved away from the trunk of the tree. She craned her neck to see the bird better.

The mockingbird shook the raindrops from his wings and flew away in the direction that the woman with the shopping bag had gone.

Peggy didn't know whether to believe her ears. But Brian said, "What did he mean by 'Look inside the tree'?"

Peggy began to look at the lumps on the trunk. One of them, near the base of the tree, had a little hole in it. Peggy bent down to look at it. "It must be a hollow tree. But this hole is too small for the cat. And it's the only hole I can see."

Brian got down on his hands and knees. He took off his mitten and poked his finger into the hole. "Peg," he said, "the bark is stretching!"

Brian wiggled his finger in the hole. It became big enough for his arm to go in. A moment later all of Brian went into the hole. The tree closed up behind him.

All Peggy could see was the little hole in the trunk of the tree.

Peggy put her hand on the lump on the tree. The bark felt cold and hard and wet. She lay down on her stomach and pushed her finger against the little hole.

The warmth of her finger seemed to melt the bark. Peggy poked her finger into the hole. Before she knew what was happening, she felt herself sucked into the tree.

It was dark inside. The only light came from the little hole in the bark. "Brian," she whispered, "where are you?"

"Here I am, Peg." Brian's voice seemed to come from down in the ground. "Watch out! There's a deep pit."

Peggy's eyes were getting used to the darkness. She felt the ground inside the tree. "I found the pit." She reached into it. "Grab my hand, Brian."

It was too dark for Peggy to see Brian. But he touched the ends of her fingers. "I can't get a grip on your hand, Peg."

Peggy turned around and poked her finger into the hole in the tree. She pushed and pushed. But the hole stayed small.

Peggy was frightened. But there was

no sense in letting Brian know it. She
took off her jacket and dangled it into
the pit. "Grab hold of this, Brian."

Peggy held onto one sleeve. And Brian grabbed the other. Peggy tried to pull her brother out of the pit. But suddenly her feet slipped from under her. The next thing she knew she was sliding into the pit.

"Look out, Brian. Here I come!"

Brian dodged to one side. Both children fell to the ground.

It took them a minute or two to get their breath back. Peggy looked up at the dim light above them. She put her jacket on. "We can't be very far under the ground. Let's dig our way out."

"That's a great idea, Peg," Brian said. "I just wish we had something to dig with."

Peggy was feeling among the roots of the tree. She pulled out two sharp stones. "Use this." She handed one of the stones to Brian.

They set to work scraping at one

side of the pit. The earth was soft and easy to dig. They just pushed it behind them.

Side by side, they scratched their way up through the ground. It was darker than anything either of them could remember. They couldn't even see the light from the little hole in the tree trunk now.

They had to dig their way between the roots of the tree. Peggy was pretending she was a mole. All of a sudden she pushed the stone she was digging with through the dirt and up into the open air.

They squirmed up out of the ground.

Brian stood up. "It's stopped raining, Peg. The sun is shining."

Peggy looked at her brother. "You're all covered with dirt. I guess I am too. Mother will have a fit."

Brian shook himself like a puppy. The dirt flew all around. A minute later Brian was no dirtier than he usually was. "This stuff comes right off."

Peggy jumped out of the way of the flying dirt. "Take it easy, Brian." She

stamped her feet and dusted the
brown earth from her clothes. She
looked down at herself. "My clothes
don't look too bad now. But my mouth
still feels gritty. And I'd like to wash
my hair."

"No reason why you can't," a voice
said. It came from the hole in the
ground that Peggy and Brian had just
come out of.

They turned to see the striped gray
cat crawl out of the hole they had dug.
The hole seemed just the right size for
the cat. "You saved me a job," he said.
"I don't much care for digging." He
flicked a clod of dirt from his tail.

"Peg, look!" Brian pointed to the hole.

While they watched, the hole got smaller and smaller. Then it was gone.

The tree looked different now. For a moment Peggy didn't know what it was. Then she said, "Brian, there are leaves on the tree, *green* leaves."

"It's hot too." Brian took off his jacket.

"Don't tell me you'd rather it was raining." The cat rolled on his back on the ground.

"Were you in the tree with us all along, Puss?" Brian asked. "Why didn't you let us know?"

"I wanted to see what you would do," the cat told him. "Not everybody can go along with the things that tree comes up with. You two did just fine." He looked at Peggy. "Didn't you say you wanted to wash your hair? Follow me."

The cat began to trot down the curving stone walk. Peggy and Brian ran after him. All the trees were covered with leaves. And the grass on each side of the walk was green.

Peggy stopped to take off her jacket and tie it around her waist. She stuffed her hat into one of the pockets. Brian was carrying his jacket. The sun was blazing down. They were glad when the cat left the walk and went around a wooded hill. It was cooler here.

On the other side of the hill a stream was tumbling straight down. It made a waterfall that splashed into a pool at the foot of the hill.

"How's that for a place to wash your hair?" The cat curled up on a flat rock in the sun and went to sleep.

Brian took off his shoes and socks and rolled up the legs of his pants. "I'm going wading. I'm sure you're not allowed to *swim* in Prospect Park."

"I don't care." Peggy wiggled out of everything but her undershirt and panties. She piled her clothes on a rock. "I never had a chance to go swimming in November before. Last one in is a rotten egg!" She jumped into the pool.

Brian was surprised that Peggy would go swimming in the park. She was usually much more careful to obey rules than he was.

"Come on in, Brian. The water is just cool enough to feel good." Peggy swam round and round in the little pool until the gritty feeling in her mouth was gone. She dived down into the clear water. Then she bobbed up to the surface to tell Brian, "There are fish swimming around in here."

Brian was still wading at the edge of the pool. He climbed out onto the mossy bank and looked all around to make sure no one was watching. Then he took off his shirt and his jeans and jumped into the water in his underwear.

The fish didn't seem to be afraid of the children. They swam so close to them that Peggy felt one glide past her cheek. She moved out of the way in a hurry. Bump! She banged into something that was jutting up out of the sand at the bottom of the pool.

Peggy came up for air. She saw Brian swimming around on his back.

"There's something stuck in the mud down there," Peggy said. "Help me dig it out."

Brian was being splashed in the face by the spray from the waterfall. He rolled onto his stomach and swam to the bottom of the pool.

Peggy pointed to an object covered with trailing waterweed. Brian pulled

off the weed. Then they tugged at
what seemed to be a small wooden
box. They had to keep coming up for
air. It was some time before they pried
the box out of the sand. Together the
children brought it to the surface.
They hauled it out of the water onto
the bank near the rock where the cat
was sleeping.

"It's heavy for such a little box. The wood must be waterlogged." Brian sat down on the moss.

Peggy splashed out of the pool. A drop of water fell on the cat's back. He uncurled himself and sat up.

The cat blinked his eyes. He stretched and jumped off the flat rock. "What've you got there?"

"A box," Brian said. "We dug it out of the bottom of the pool."

The cat's ears perked up. And the end of his tail twitched. "What's in it?"

Brian tried to open the box. "It's rusted shut." He shook it. Something rattled inside. "If we take it home with us I could pry it open with a screwdriver."

Peggy jumped to her feet. "Home!" she said. "We'd better go home. I wonder what time it is." Peggy didn't take time to let herself get dry in the sun. She started to pull her clothes on over her wet underwear.

Brian rushed to get dressed too. He tucked the box under his arm. "Come on, Puss."

"I know a shortcut," the cat said. He began to climb straight up the hill beside the waterfall.

The children had a hard time keeping up with him. There was no path. Their feet skidded on the steep slope. The dirt and stones gave way under them. The day was very warm. Peggy and Brian didn't mind that their underwear was wet. It helped to keep them cool.

"Peg," Brian said when they were close to the top of the hill. "I never knew there was such a high hill in Prospect Park."

Peggy didn't answer right away. She'd been wondering where all the people were who were always in the park on a sunny Saturday. Ever since she saw the green leaves on the trees, a strange thought had come to her. She didn't know why she wasn't frightened by it. But she wasn't.

They had reached the top of the hill. Peggy looked out over green meadows. There was no sign of the tall buildings that were all around Prospect Park. Instead Peggy saw something that made her grab Brian's arm. "Look! Now I'm sure we're not really in the park at all!"

Beyond the meadows there was a wood. And from the middle of the wood rose the gray stone towers of a castle.

Brian stared at the castle. Then he said, "We've just got to explore it, Peg." He called to the cat, "Puss, wait a minute."

The cat was about to start down the other side of the hill. He turned around to look at the children. "Come along. I'm hungry. Your mother must be fixing lunch."

"I want to go and see the castle over there." Brian pointed to it.

"It's not a good time now," the cat said.

Peggy had read stories about castles. And she'd often wished she lived in one. She wondered what was inside the stone towers. "Can you take us some other time, Puss?" she asked.

The cat looked at her for a minute with his green eyes. He smoothed his whiskers with one paw. "I'd be glad to," he said. "Now, come along." He started down the other side of the hill.

Peggy took the heavy box from Brian. "I'll carry it for a while."

They followed the cat down the hill and along the stone walk to the old beech tree.

Peggy put on her jacket. She got down on her knees and held the wooden box in her arms. Then she rammed her head against the hole in the tree trunk. The bark of the tree began to stretch. A moment later Peggy was inside the tree.

Brian pushed his way in after her. Then the cat joined the two children.

"What are we waiting for?" Puss jumped into the pit.

Brian climbed down by holding onto one of the thick tree roots that grew at the sides of the pit. "Hand me the box, Peg."

Peggy leaned over the edge to give him the wooden box. Then she grabbed a root and lowered herself into the pit.

"What'll we use to dig with?" Peggy asked.

Brian started to scrape at the dirt with a corner of the box he was holding. "Look, Peg. The ground is opening up!"

Puss rubbed against Peggy's ankle. She picked him up. By the dim light from the hole in the tree the children and the cat saw the earth crumbling away.

In a few moments a little hole

appeared at one end of a tunnel. The hole grew larger. And so did the tunnel. In no time at all Peggy and Brian could walk out into the open air.

They were back in the park. The rain was coming down hard now. Peggy put the cat on the ground so she could hold the wooden box. Brian put on his jacket and pulled his cap down over his ears.

"Hurry up." Puss raced down the stone walk toward the park gate.

The wet underwear didn't feel at all good now. Brian started to run after the cat.

Peggy turned to look back. The big hole had vanished. And the ground around the tree was covered with fallen leaves.

Mrs. Dobson was looking out of the window at the rain. She opened the front door before Peggy had a chance to ring the doorbell.

"Come in, children," she said. "You must be soaked to the skin. Run upstairs and get out of those wet clothes." She leaned over to pet the cat. "Poor Puss. Come into the kitchen and get something to eat."

Mr. Dobson walked into the hall. "I see we're still stuck with that cat. Couldn't you find his owner?"

"She ran away when she saw us." Peggy started up the stairs to change her clothes. Brian went up after her.

When lunch was over, the two children took the wooden box to their father's workbench in the basement.

Peggy thought it might help to oil the hinges. But still the box wouldn't open.

"Maybe it's nailed shut." Brian held the box right under the light bulb over the workbench. The wood was so dark from being underwater that he couldn't see if there were nails in it. "I'll use a hammer and screwdriver to crack it open."

Brian banged and pried. He even tried to saw the box in half. But the wood was so hard that the saw didn't even scratch it.

Brian put down the saw. "It's no use, Peg. I can't get it open."

Peggy looked at the box. "Brian, I have an idea. But we'll have to go back to the park to try it."

"It's snowing now. Puss won't want to go out in this weather," Brian said. "He's in the living room with Dad, watching television."

Peggy picked up the box. "We'll go without him."

"Our jackets are still wet," Brian said.

"We'll find something," Peggy told him.

Their mother didn't even look up when the children walked through the kitchen. Mrs. Dobson was busy chopping onions to stuff a chicken. And onions always made her eyes water.

Peggy took her new winter coat out of the hall closet. She put on rubber boots and a knitted cap. Brian borrowed her old ski jacket. It was too small for Peggy, and it was a little big on Brian. But it would have to do. He found a pair of fuzzy red earmuffs in one pocket and mittens in the other.

While Brian got into his boots, Peggy ran up to her room for her new gloves.

Peggy and Brian took the wooden

box and went quietly out the front door. They ran all the way to the park. The snow was coming down in fat flakes that stuck to their eyelashes. The air was so cold that their breath came out like steam.

"I know what your idea is, Peg," Brian said. "You think the magic tree can open the box for us."

Peggy nodded. "It's worth a try."

They were walking along the stone path. The snow underfoot kept their feet from making any noise.

Brian peered through the falling snowflakes. "Look," he whispered.

Peggy saw someone in a brown coat walking ahead of them. "It's the lady with the shopping bag."

"There's something funny about her. Let's sneak up and see what she's up to." Brian pulled Peggy away from the walk.

The children ducked behind the trees. They moved from one tree to the next. The woman in the brown coat sat down on the bench near the lumpy old beech tree. She started fumbling around in her shopping bag.

Peggy and Brian ran over and hid behind the tree.

Peggy and Brian stood close together behind the beech tree. The woman in the brown coat sat on the bench on the other side.

Peggy leaned against the trunk. "She might see us if we looked around the tree."

Brian pointed to the branches overhead. "She wouldn't be likely to look up there. It's an easy tree to climb, Peg. I'll go first. You can hand the box up to me."

"I might tear my coat," Peggy said.

"I wish we could get up into the tree without having to climb."

Suddenly Peggy felt herself slowly rising in the air. She looked at Brian. He was floating up beside her.

Peggy held the wooden box under one arm. She reached out to grab Brian's hand.

"Don't touch me, Peg," he whispered. "I might go pop. I feel like a gas balloon."

They sailed up among the branches of the tree and stopped. Peggy sat down on a thick branch. Now she felt just as heavy as ever. Brian sat down beside her. He pointed to the woman below them.

She was pulling the blue tablecloth out of her shopping bag. The woman leaned over the cloth and said something to it. At once the cloth gave a little shake and spread itself on the walk at the woman's feet.

Peggy and Brian saw that a place was set for dinner on the tablecloth. There were pretty dishes with blue flowers on them and shining silverware.

The woman got off the bench. She sat down on the ground and started to eat a bowl of steaming stew. The snowflakes were falling all around her. But they never seemed to get into the stew.

There was a plate of crusty rolls that smelled as if they had just come out of the oven. The woman ate them with the stew. When she'd had all she wanted, she clapped her hands.

The dirty dishes vanished. In their place was a thick wedge of apple pie and a cup of hot chocolate. The smell was wonderful.

After she was all done, the woman wiped her mouth on a blue napkin. Again she clapped her hands. All the dishes disappeared. The tablecloth folded itself up. Then the woman put it back into the shopping bag. She got to her feet and walked away through the park.

"I read about something like that in a book," Peggy said. "It's a great way to have a picnic."

"But why would she want to eat outdoors when it's snowing?" Brian asked. "Let's follow her and find out where she's going."

Peggy looked at the wooden box on her lap. "We don't want to forget why we came to the tree."

They heard a chirp from the branch above them. Peggy and Brian looked up to see the mockingbird perched overhead. He was all fluffed out like a ball of gray feathers.

All of a sudden the bird hopped down onto the box on Peggy's lap. She was so surprised she almost dropped it.

The mockingbird tapped the box with his beak. "What do you have in here?"

"We don't know," Brian said. "We can't get it open."

"I thought the tree might help us open the box," Peggy told the bird. "I wish it would."

"If I were a woodpecker, maybe I

could help you." The mockingbird gave the box a peck. Then he fluttered up onto Brian's shoulder.

The box slid off Peggy's lap and fell through the branches of the tree. It crashed against the stone bench and bounced to the ground.

"I'm sorry," the bird said. "I must have kicked it during take-off." He flew down to the box. "Anyway, it did the trick. Your box is open now."

Brian started to scramble down the tree. Peggy came slowly after him. She was careful not to rip her coat.

When Brian reached the foot of the tree, he ran over to the box. "It's cracked in half, Peg. And it's empty. Whatever was in it must have fallen out."

Brian looked on the ground around the box. "There's so much snow it's hard to find anything. Of course, it would help if we knew what we were looking for."

The mockingbird was hopping around on the ground by the bench. He picked up something shiny and flew up into the tree to show it to Peggy. She was sitting on the bottom branch now.

The bird perched on a twig near Peggy. She took the object out of his beak. It was the ring from a pop-top can. "People are always dropping these in the park," she said.

The mockingbird stared at the ground. "I have very sharp eyes. I just wish I knew what you were looking for."

A second later the bird gave a chirp. He dived down and pulled something out of the snow.

Brian glanced at it. "Another ring from a pop-top can."

Peggy had climbed down from the tree. The bird fluttered over to her and perched on her shoulder. She took the shiny thing out of his beak.

"Brian," she said. "Maybe this *is* what was in the box."

Brian came over to see.

Peggy was holding a little key. It was different from any they had ever seen. The handle was all carved with fancy designs. And the key was the same color as their mother's wedding ring.

"It must be made of gold," Peggy said. "I'd better take care of it." She put the key into the pocket of her coat.

"I wonder where the lady with the shopping bag went," Brian said.

The mockingbird was perched on the bottom branch of the beech tree. "If you follow me, I can show you." He fluttered over to a tree on the other side of the walk.

Brian was cold from standing still. He was glad to run after the bird.

Peggy dropped the pop-top ring into a trash basket beside the stone bench. She picked up the broken pieces of the wooden box and threw them into the basket too. Then she went after her brother.

The mockingbird flew from tree to tree in the park. At each tree he stopped to wait for Brian and Peggy to catch up with him.

They crossed the highway that went around the park. There was no traffic on it today. Cars were not allowed in the park on weekends.

The snow was still falling. Brian and Peggy followed the bird across a broad meadow to the shore of a lake.

"Look, Peg." Brian pointed to the ice forming at the edge of the water. "It's starting to freeze."

The mockingbird flew close to the lake. Brian and Peggy walked along the stone wall that rimmed the shore. They passed the place where the yellow water lilies bloomed in the summertime. Now they were just a tangle of brown stems in the water.

At one point the lake was narrow.

An old iron bridge arched over it. The bird swooped down and flew under the bridge. Peggy and Brian followed him.

Close against the side of the arch they saw the woman in the brown coat. She had spread a layer of newspapers on the ground and was sitting on them. The snow could not fall on her here.

The mockingbird flew down onto the newspapers.

"Oh, there you are, my pretty!" the woman said. "And you want your supper, don't you?" She reached into the shopping bag and took out the blue tablecloth. Then she caught sight of Brian and Peggy.

The woman quickly stuffed the cloth back into the shopping bag. She jumped to her feet. Peggy thought she looked frightened.

"What do you want?" The woman looked around at the shadowy places under the bridge. "Is that cat with you?"

"No." Brian walked over to her. "He doesn't like nasty weather."

"We thought he was your cat," Peggy said.

"Oh no." The woman blew on her hands. They were red with cold. "I don't trust that cat," she said.

"What cat can you trust?" the mockingbird chirped.

The woman didn't seem to understand the bird. "I'll give you something to eat in a little while, lovey." She grabbed the handles of the shopping bag to hold it shut. "Isn't it time you children went home for supper?"

"Are *you* going to stay *here*?" Brian asked.

"I like it better than the subway station," the woman told him.

"Oh," Peggy said, "don't you have a home?"

The woman shook her head. "Not anymore."

"What do you sleep on?" Peggy wanted to know.

The woman pointed to the news-papers. "These are nice and dry."

"I have a sleeping bag," Peggy said. "I'll lend it to you."

"No, no, dear. I'm sure your mother wouldn't like that." The woman patted Peggy's arm. "Don't worry about me. Old Annie will be all right."

"Is that your name — Annie?" Brian asked. "Can we call you that? Aren't you Mrs. Something or other?"

"Just call me Annie." The woman smiled. "And what are your names?"

"I'm Brian. And this is my sister, Peggy. I call her Peg."

The mockingbird flew onto a ledge under the bridge. "Peggy," he chirped. "I'm hungry. And I can see she's never going to feed me as long as you're here."

The woman looked up at the bird. "He keeps me company. Don't you, lovey?"

"We have to go home," Peggy said.

"Good-bye, Annie." Brian walked out from under the bridge.

"Good-bye." Annie waved to the two children.

Peggy and Brian ran back along the lake shore. They took a shortcut over a hill and across the highway to the gate of the park.

Then they crossed the wide street and walked the two blocks to their house.

Brian rang the doorbell. Mr. Dobson opened the front door. Puss ran to the door. He looked out at the falling snow.

The children walked into the house. Peggy went to the hall closet. She hung up her coat and put away her boots.

Brian sat down on the bottom step of the stairs to pull off his boots. "How was the game, Dad?"

"Great!" Mr. Dobson leaned over to pet the cat.

Mrs. Dobson was coming downstairs with a basket of laundry. "I thought you didn't like Puss, George."

"A cat who roots for the Navy team

can't be all bad," Mr. Dobson said.

Mrs. Dobson laughed. "I suppose he did somersaults when Navy made a touchdown."

"Not quite." Mr. Dobson petted the cat again.

"What did Puss do, Dad?" Brian unzipped the ski jacket and went to hang it in the closet.

"He hissed the referee when he gave Navy a penalty. And I never heard any cat purr as loud as this one did when Navy won the game." Mr. Dobson took the basket. "I'll carry this down to the laundry room for you, Helen."

Mrs. Dobson looked at Brian and Peggy. "I see you two were out in the weather again."

"We talked to the lady in the park," Peggy told her mother. "She said Puss doesn't belong to her."

"Who do you belong to, Puss?" Mrs. Dobson asked.

The cat just rubbed against her legs and purred.

"I'd better get busy with supper." Mrs. Dobson walked to the kitchen.

As soon as their parents had gone, Brian sat down on the floor beside the cat. "You sure got yourself in good with Dad."

The cat smoothed his whiskers. He looked at Peggy. "What did you do with the box you found this morning?"

"We couldn't get it open," Peggy said. "So we took it to the magic tree."

"That was a good idea," the cat said. "I wonder why I didn't think of it. Did the tree get it open?"

"Yes," Brian told him.

"What was in it?" Puss asked.

"We're not sure," Peggy said. "The box fell out of the tree and broke. The mockingbird found a key in the snow near it. But we're not certain that's what was in the box."

"Where's the key?" the cat wanted to know.

Peggy went to the hall closet and took the little golden key out of the pocket of her coat. She bent down to show it to the cat.

Puss looked at the key. Then he sniffed it. His tail twitched. And he began to paw the ground. "No wonder nobody could find that key! It's been at the bottom of the pool for ages."

"You mean you know about this key?" Brian asked.

Puss nodded. His green eyes gleamed.

"What does it unlock?" Peggy said.

"I'll show you," the cat promised, "just as soon as it stops snowing."

After supper Peggy worked on her math. She wasn't very good at fractions. It was after nine-thirty when she finished. Brian was already in bed.

Peggy took a quick shower. Almost as soon as her head touched the pillow, she fell asleep.

During the night Peggy dreamed that she was a very little girl again. She had been eating bread and jam. And her mother was scrubbing her face with a washcloth.

Peggy woke up. The cat was licking her face with his rough tongue.

"Ouch!" Peggy sat up in bed. "What do you want, Puss?"

"It's stopped snowing," the cat said. "You wanted to see what the golden key unlocks."

Peggy snuggled under the covers. "Can't we wait until tomorrow morning?"

The cat jumped off Peggy's bed and ran to the window. He grabbed the venetian-blind cord in his teeth and pulled up the blind. At once the room was filled with moonlight.

"There's a full moon tonight," the cat said. "It's the best time to visit the castle."

The castle! Peggy remembered the stone towers rising against the sky. She threw off the covers and put on her bathrobe and slippers. Then she tiptoed down the hall in the dark to Brian's room.

"Wake up!" she whispered in her brother's ear.

Brian turned over and dragged the blanket over his head.

Peggy shook him. "Hurry up! We're going to see the castle!"

Brian poked his head out from under the blanket. "What did you say?"

"Puss says the best time to go to the castle is when the moon is full," Peggy

told him. "Put your clothes on, Brian."

Brian slipped out from under the covers. "Good thing Mom put our wet jackets in the clothes dryer."

"Sh-sh! We don't want to wake Mother and Daddy." Peggy went back to her own room to get dressed.

Brian had given Peggy a little flashlight for her birthday. She took it out of her dresser drawer and used it to light the way down the stairs when she went to get her hat and jacket.

Brian came down while she was pulling on her rubber boots. "It's warm where we're going," he reminded her.

"We still have to walk through the park," Peggy said.

Puss was sitting on the bannister post in the front hall waiting for them. "I hate getting snow on my paws. Would you mind carrying me?"

When they were ready to go out, Brian picked up the cat. Peggy turned off the flashlight. She tucked it into her pocket beside the golden key. Then she quietly opened the door and stepped out onto the moonlit front stoop of the house.

Brian and the cat came after her.

Brian and Peggy and the cat were all alone on the snowy Brooklyn street. No one had shoveled the sidewalk. And the snowplow had not yet come by. The children picked their way through the drifts. In some places the snow was higher than their boot tops.

It wasn't until they were crossing the wide street by the park that Peggy remembered what her mother said: "Prospect Park is not safe after dark."

Peggy knew she ought to turn around and go home. But she wanted so much to see the inside of the castle. Brian seemed to have forgotten their mother's warning. Peggy decided not to remind him.

They went into the park by the gate. The ground was hidden under the snow. But they could tell where the walk was by the old-fashioned lamp posts and the stone benches placed here and there. The twigs and branches of the bare trees were icy. They sparkled in the lamplight.

Peggy and Brian walked toward the old beech. Long before they reached it, they heard the lilting song of the mockingbird. He was perched on a branch close to the top of the tree.

When the children came near the tree, the bird stopped singing and fluttered down. Peggy thought he was going to land on her shoulder. But when the bird saw the cat Brian was carrying, he flew up and perched on a low branch of the tree. "What are you doing here at this time of night?" he chirped.

"We're going to the magic country where it's summertime," Brian told the bird.

The mockingbird cocked his head to look down at them. "Is that where the box came from?"

"Yes," Peggy said. "Thank you for finding the key for us."

Suddenly the cat jumped out of Brian's arms. He landed at the foot of the tree. At once the mockingbird flew to a tree on the other side of the walk. He perched there to watch what was going on.

Puss jammed his pink nose into the little hole in the tree trunk. His head went in, and then his shoulders. Soon only the end of his striped tail was sticking out. Then that too was gone.

Brian dived after the cat. The hole in the tree seemed to open up and swallow him.

Peggy got down on her hands and knees. She poked her finger into the hole in the bark. "I wish you could come too," she said to the mocking-bird. "But you wouldn't like digging through a lot of dirt. I wish there were some other way." She took one last look at the bird. Then she pushed her way into the tree.

Peggy found herself inside the tree. It was dark. She took out her flashlight and turned it on. The pit was right in front of her. Brian and the cat were already down in it.

Peggy shone the flashlight between two thick tree roots at the side of the pit. "Look, Brian!"

"It's a little door!" Brian wiggled between the roots. "But there's no handle on it, Peg. And it's locked."

The cat looked up at Peggy. "Don't you have your key?"

Peggy climbed down one of the roots into the pit. She took the gold key out of her pocket and gave it to her brother.

Brian stooped down to fit it into a keyhole in the door. He gave the key a turn. The lock clicked. And the door opened inward.

Puss squeezed between Brian's legs and stuck his head through the little doorway. He sniffed the air inside. "All clear." He walked through the door.

The door was just big enough for Brian and Peggy to crawl through. Brian went first, with the flashlight. Peggy took the key out of the door and put it back into her pocket. Then she followed Brian.

Just inside the door a flight of steps led upward. The cat climbed the steps. Peggy and Brian went after him.

A faint light came from above. Brian turned off the flashlight and handed it back to Peggy.

At the top of the steps they came out of the ground. Peggy looked around. They were outdoors in the moonlight. The air was filled with the smell of clover. A dirt road led through a meadow to a wood. And high over the wood the children could see the towers of the castle.

It was too warm now to wear their jackets. They stuffed their hats and mittens in the pockets and tied the jackets around their waists.

Puss was already walking along the road. Brian and Peggy rushed to keep up.

They walked around a deep hole. A little farther along they came to another one on the other side of the road. The children had to zig-zag between holes all the way to the wood.

The road sloped upward. The woods were on the sides of a hill. And the castle was built on the top.

After a while the road wound between the trees. There were dark shadows here. Brian and Peggy had to be careful not to fall into the holes in the road.

They followed the cat up and up. At last they came to a high stone wall with towers along it. The wall was covered with ivy. The cat climbed from one stone to the next. Brian and Peggy followed him up the wall. They wedged their feet between the stones and grabbed hold of the ivy for support. Their rubber boots made it hard to climb. But they kept on going.

Just before they reached the top of the wall, Peggy looked back at the road over the meadow. The deep holes made dark patches in the moonlight. From here Peggy could see the shape of them. "Brian, look!"

Brian looked where she was pointing. "Peg," he said, "those aren't ordinary holes. They're footprints!"

"Maybe we ought to go back," Peggy whispered.

"I guess you're right," Brian agreed. "Those footprints are scary." He poked his head over the top of the wall. "Wow!"

Peggy peeked over the wall too.

The castle rose in front of them. A full moon floated over it. And all the towers and turrets gleamed in the moonlight.

It was so beautiful that both children forgot everything else. They climbed up onto the thick wall. There was a road around the top. Brian and Peggy crossed the road and looked down the other side of the wall.

The castle was surrounded by a deep trench. A drawbridge went over it.

"That looks as if it used to be a moat," Peggy said. "But somebody has made it into a garden."

The moonlight glistened on a stream that wound through the center of the trench. Tall hollyhocks bloomed on one side of the stream. Five fruit trees grew on the other. Peggy saw a bed of cabbages. There were roses climbing over the drawbridge. And a honeysuckle vine was starting to grow up the side of the castle.

Puss was waiting for them by one of the towers in the thick wall. Peggy and Brian walked toward the cat. When he saw them coming, he ran into the tower. The children followed him.

They went down a winding stone stair inside the dark tower. At the foot of the stair a door opened into the moonlit garden.

Puss went quietly across the wooden drawbridge. Peggy and Brian tiptoed after him.

On the other side of the bridge they came to two stone towers. There was a heavy wooden door between them. Brian gave the door a shove. It swung open.

Puss ran through an archway into an open courtyard. Peggy and Brian slipped in behind him.

They looked around. There were buildings in the courtyard. Peggy peeked into a long, low shed. It was dark inside. She turned on her flashlight. "Look at the stalls in there."

"It must be a stable," Brian said. "But where are the horses?"

In another building they saw a big brick oven. It looked as if it hadn't been used for a long time.

The cat led them across the courtyard to the main building of the castle. There were towers on the corners. Turrets with pointed roofs jutted into the sky.

Puss walked over to a great door in the side of the castle. It had iron hinges and a big iron lock. Peggy tried the handle of the door. "It's locked."

"Use your key," the cat said.

Peggy felt sure the key was much too small for the lock. But she didn't want to argue. She poked the little golden key into the big keyhole.

Click! The door opened.

Peggy and Brian followed Puss into a dark hallway.

As soon as he was inside the castle, Puss turned and ran up a curving stairway. Peggy and Brian went after him. The moonlight came through narrow slits in the thick stone walls.

Puss ducked into a little round room. The children saw a four-poster bed and a large carved wardrobe. The cat poked his nose under the bed and all around the shadowy room. Peggy turned on the flashlight. And Brian opened the wardrobe for Puss to look into it.

"Not here." The cat ran out of the room and raced farther up the winding stairs to a room higher in the tower.

Brian and Peggy followed him from room to room. They went up one stairway and down the next. Everywhere the cat kept searching.

"What are you looking for, Puss?" Brian asked.

"I'll show you when I find it," the cat said.

Nobody seemed to be living in any of the rooms. They were covered with dust. There were cobwebs on the stairs. And mice scampered out of the way of the cat.

"There's one more place to look," the cat said. He went down a stairway.

Peggy and Brian walked down after him. At the bottom of the stairs they came to a hallway. Light glowed from an open doorway at one end of it. And they could hear a loud buzzing noise.

The two children followed the cat down the hallway. The buzzing got louder and louder. They stepped through the doorway into a large room with a high ceiling.

The stone floor was covered with animal skins. Beautiful pictures on cloth hung on the walls. Between the pictures there were shields and spears. The light came from a fire blazing in a great stone fireplace at the far end of the room.

There were heavy benches and chairs along the sides of the room. And down the center was a long, long table.

"What's that?" Brian pointed to a mound of cloth on the table. The mound was so big that it went from one end of the table to the other.

Suddenly the mound stirred.

"It's alive!" Peggy whispered.

The next thing they knew, an enormous hand moved over to the edge of the table. And a huge foot dangled over the end.

The buzzing stopped. Peggy and Brian heard a snort. Then the steady buzzing sound began again.

A giant was lying on the table. He was asleep and snoring.

"Let's get out of here, Peg." Brian started for the door.

Peggy went after him.

Puss came running over. "You can't go now," he said. "I've found it at last."

"You mean what you were looking for all over the castle?" Brian asked.

"Yes," the cat told him. "And I need Peggy to open it with her key."

Peggy took a look at the long table. The giant had rolled over onto his side. His cheek rested on his enormous hand. He had stopped snoring, but his eyes were closed. And he seemed to be fast asleep.

The cat trotted across the room to a small black leather chest which stood against one of the walls. The chest had fancy brass corners and a carved brass lock.

Peggy and Brian tiptoed across the room to look at the chest. Peggy bent down and put the golden key into the lock. She gave it a turn, and the lock opened.

Peggy pulled out the key and put it back into her pocket. Brian lifted the lid of the chest.

Puss stood on his hind legs and rested his paws on the edge of the chest. He looked inside. Peggy and Brian leaned over the cat.

It was dark inside the chest.

"Use your flashlight, Peg," Brian whispered.

She clicked it on. Now they could see that the inside of the chest was lined in red leather. But there wasn't anything in it.

The cat stared. "It's empty!" he wailed.

"Of course," a loud voice boomed. "What did you expect?"

Peggy's heart seemed to stop beating. She turned to look at the giant. He was sitting up on the table. His head nearly touched the rafters of the tall room. Peggy saw a sharp dagger in the giant's belt.

"Turn off the flashlight, Peg," Brian said softly.

Peggy's hand was shaking so much that she could hardly click the switch. Brian began to pull her toward the door.

"Keep close to the wall, Brian,"

Peggy whispered. "Maybe the giant will think we're part of one of the pictures."

The children moved inch by inch closer to the door. All the while they could hear the cat talking to the giant.

"Puss is keeping him busy so we can sneak out," Brian said.

The giant raised his voice. Peggy put her hands over her ears. But still she could hear him. He sounded angry.

"Where have you been all this time?" the giant thundered.

Puss started walking toward the door. "Don't get excited. I can explain everything."

The giant rolled off the long table. There wasn't room for him to stand up. He got down on his hands and knees and started to crawl after the cat.

Puss ran past Brian and Peggy and

streaked out the door. They started after him.

The giant stretched out his long arm and grabbed the two children. They tried to jump out of his hand. But no matter how they struggled, they couldn't get away.

Peggy and Brian looked up into the giant's face. He had green eyes and a scraggly red beard and the biggest freckles they had ever seen.

"Please don't run away," the giant thundered. "I want to talk to you."

Brian put his hands over his ears. "Please don't talk so loud!"

"Oh, I'm sorry," the giant said in a much smaller voice. "I keep forgetting. Is this better?"

"Yes, thank you," Peggy said. "And please don't hold us so tight. I can hardly breathe."

"Why don't you sit here?" The giant set the children down on top of the long table. He lay on the floor beside it and rested on one elbow.

Peggy and Brian hung their legs over the edge of the table and looked up at the giant.

"I would offer you something to eat," he said. "But I've eaten everything I cooked for supper. It's a bother to be so big. Just shelling enough peas takes me all day."

"So that's what happened to the people and the horses who used to live in the castle!" Brian said. "I guess if you're hungry enough you'll eat anything."

Peggy felt a chill run down her back. How could Brian say such things? Now the giant really would be angry.

But the giant just stared at Brian. "That must have been what everybody thought," he said. "They all ran away when I got to be this size. Only Puss stayed to keep me company. And now he's gone."

Peggy thought she saw a tear start in one of the giant's enormous green eyes. But he blinked it away and smiled. "I'm glad the cat is all right. I was worried about him."

Peggy wasn't afraid anymore. "What do you mean about getting to be this size?" she asked. "Weren't you always this big?"

"A year ago I was about the same size as any other man," the giant told her.

Brian looked around. "Then that's why the castle is too small for you."

Peggy stood up. "Did you eat something that made you grow?"

"No. It happened all at once," the giant said. "I was trying to get Puss out of a tree. He had climbed all the way to the top and was stuck there. I was tired and didn't feel like climbing up after the cat. But suddenly I was so tall I could just pick him out of the branches."

The giant tried to stretch his arms and legs. He had to be careful not to bump into the walls. "Do you mind if we go outdoors? I'd like to stand up." He started to crawl toward the doorway of the big room.

Peggy and Brian jumped off the table and walked after him.

The giant lay on his stomach and slid through the hall and out of the door to the courtyard. Then he stood up. Peggy and Brian came out after him into the moonlight.

It felt good to be in the open air again.

The giant crossed the courtyard. He looked at the stable. "There's no use my keeping horses now." He ducked

under the archway between the stone
towers. The children ran to keep up
with him.

When he reached the garden, the
giant bent down to smell the roses. He
saw something hiding under the
drawbridge. The giant picked it up
between his thumb and forefinger.

It was the cat.

"Take it easy, Fred! I told you I could explain everything." Puss wiggled between the giant's fingers.

The giant stood up. He put the cat on the palm of his hand. "You ran out without introducing me to your friends. I see they found the key my father hid. What were you looking for in the leather chest?"

"I was just trying to help you, Fred," the cat said. "Somebody once told me there was something in that chest that would keep anybody from going hungry."

"At one time I used to keep my tablecloth in the chest. That was before I met you, Puss," the giant said. "But I got tired of locking and unlocking it. So I put the tablecloth in the bottom drawer of the sideboard. I thought everybody would think it was still in the chest. You were the only one who knew where it was." The giant scratched his beard. "But now I can't find the tablecloth anywhere."

"Was it blue?" Brian asked.

The giant looked down at him. "What do you know about it?"

Puss interrupted. "This is Brian. And this is his sister, Peggy."

The giant picked Brian off the ground and set him on top of the wall that ran around the castle. Now he was as high as the giant's head. "What do you know about the tablecloth, Brian?"

"I met somebody who has a magic

tablecloth that covers itself with food," Brian told him. "Is that what you lost?"

Peggy was still on the ground at the giant's feet. She was afraid he might step on her. She climbed onto his shoe. "Fred," she called up to him, "Annie *needs* the tablecloth."

Puss arched his back and stretched his neck to look up at the giant. "That's what I thought when I lent it to her."

Fred bent down to pick up Peggy. He put her on the wall beside Brian.

But he held onto the cat. "It sounds as if you have a story to tell, Puss. Let's hear it."

"Annie didn't have a place to stay or anything to eat. I lent her the tablecloth for a day or two," the cat said. "Now she doesn't want to give it back. I thought there was something in

the leather chest that you could use instead. Then Annie could keep the tablecloth."

"If I had something in the chest, why wouldn't I open it and use it?" Fred asked.

"I thought you didn't have the key." Puss smoothed his whiskers. "What was all the talk about the golden key your father hid?"

"My father said that key could cause trouble — if the wrong person got hold of it," Fred told him.

"You mean you have a different key to the leather chest?" the cat said.

"Of course. But it's just an ordinary key." Fred put the cat on the wall beside the children. "You're not a bad cat, Puss," he said. "But you certainly have made a mess of things."

"What happened to your moat, Fred?" Brian asked.

"Moats are used to keep enemies out," the giant said. "But my father didn't have any enemies. He was always making friends. One dry summer there wasn't enough water in the mill stream down there." Fred pointed to the meadows at the foot of the hill. "So my father let most of the water in the moat flow into the mill stream. Then the mill wheel turned. And the miller could grind the farmers' grain into flour."

"Is the mill still there?" Peggy asked. "I'd like to see it."

"The mill is there. But the miller is

afraid of me now that I'm so big," the giant said. "I don't often go into the meadows anymore."

Peggy thought he sounded sad. She changed the subject. "You have a beautiful garden. Who planted it?"

"I did," Fred told her. "I like to grow things."

Brian looked at the rows of cabbages. "It's lucky you planted vegetables. You have something to eat even though you don't have the magic tablecloth anymore."

"I'm waiting for my apples to ripen." The giant looked at the children. "Do you like cherries?"

"Cherries! I *love* cherries," Peggy said.

"So do I." Brian looked down into the garden. "Which is the cherry tree?"

The giant picked up Brian with one

hand and Peggy with the other. He turned around and leaned over the trees growing on the bank of the stream.

Peggy clicked on her flashlight and shone it into the branches. She saw apples on two of the trees and pears on another. Little green peaches grew on the fourth tree. And the fifth was loaded with cherries.

"You look like a firefly with that magic lamp of yours, Peggy." The giant held the children close to the branches of the cherry tree.

Peggy climbed into a crotch of the tree. She shone the flashlight on a cluster of cherries that hung just over her head. Peggy picked one and popped it into her mouth. "Yum!"

Brian was sitting on a thick branch. "It looks as if every one of them is ripe, Fred. Why don't you eat them?"

"My fingers are so big," the giant told him, "that I squash the cherries when I try to pick them."

"I'll pick some for you, Fred," Peggy said.

"That's nice of you, Peggy. But you'd have to pick cherries all night to get enough to make one mouthful for me." The giant sat down cross-legged beside the tree. "It's fun for me just to see you eat them."

Puss was still on the stone wall. He watched Brian and Peggy stuffing themselves with cherries. All at once there was a whirr of wings. A bird dived out of the sky. When it saw the cat, the bird flew up again.

Peggy thought she heard someone calling her name. "Here I am," she cried from the tree.

The bird flew down toward her. Now Peggy saw that it was the mockingbird.

"Come quickly," the bird called. "Annie needs you!"

The bird was flying around and around the cherry tree. He seemed to want Peggy and Brian to follow him.

The giant stood up. "It would be faster if I carried you," he said to the children. "Would you mind sitting on my head? I'm sorry my hair is such a mess. I don't have the right size comb. I tried using a rake. But even that wasn't big enough."

"Hurry!" the bird cried.

Fred picked Brian and Peggy out of the cherry tree and put them on his head. Then he lifted the cat off the wall and set him beside the children.

"Hold tight." The giant climbed over
the stone wall and strode along the dirt
road that led down the hill.

Brian and Peggy grabbed onto the
giant's hair and tried to keep from
bouncing up and down.

"It's like going on a hayride," Brian said.

Peggy held the cat on her lap. "Just don't use your claws to hang on," she told him.

The giant's head was higher than the trees in the woods on the side of the hill. He walked almost as fast as the mockingbird could fly.

They crossed the meadows and followed the bird over a line of low hills. Peggy pointed ahead of them. "Look, Brian, there's the magic tree."

The giant stopped walking. He stared at the beech tree. "Puss, that looks like the tree you were stuck in."

The mockingbird flew to the tree and perched on one of the branches. Fred reached up and took the children and the cat off his head. He put them on the ground near the tree.

Puss dived at the little hole in the

trunk and pushed his way into the tree. Brian went after the cat.

The bird flew down to the hole. Then he flew back up to the branch.

"Why don't you go into the tree?" Peggy asked.

"A cat's a cat," the mockingbird said. "I don't want to be too close to one."

Peggy got down on all fours. She put her hand on the lumpy trunk. "I wish you and Puss could be friends," she said to the bird.

At once the mockingbird flew down to the little hole. He poked his beak in. Then all the rest of him went in until only his tail feathers stuck out. In a second they too were gone.

The giant watched the bird. "If only I were the size I used to be, I'd go too. But it's your turn now, Peggy. You'd better go."

Peggy pushed her finger into the

hole in the trunk. "I wish you could come with us, Fred." The bark stretched big enough for Peggy's arm to go in. Soon her head was inside the tree. And then all of Peggy was in.

It was very dark. Peggy turned on her flashlight. She looked into the pit. Brian and the cat were there. And so was the mockingbird. He was perched on the cat's back. And Puss was purring.

Peggy looked at the cat and the bird. "I see you two decided to get along with each other after all." She began to climb down the tree roots into the pit.

All at once Peggy heard a noise over her head. She held onto a root and shone her flashlight up at the little hole she had come in by. "Brian, look!"

The hole was stretching. An arm poked through from outside. Someone else was coming into the tree!

Peggy held her breath. She watched an arm, then a shoulder, and then the top of a shaggy head come through the hole. Before Peggy could switch off the flashlight, a man had squeezed through the tree trunk. He pulled his foot out of the hole. And the hole closed up to its usual size. The man stood up.

Suddenly the cat became so excited that he leaped up out of the pit onto the ledge above. Puss forgot that the mockingbird was perched on his back.

The bird flew onto a root. "Next time tell me before you do something like that. You made me bend a wing feather."

Puss didn't answer. He was too busy rubbing against the leg of the man on the ledge. "Oh, Fred!" he said. "You're back to the right size. How did you do it?"

Now Peggy and Brian saw that the

man on the ledge was the giant — only he wasn't a giant anymore. He wasn't any taller than their father.

"What happened, Fred?" Brian asked.

For a minute, Fred didn't answer. He looked dazed. "I just touched the little hole in the tree trunk, and before I knew it I was in here with you."

"Don't forget why we're here," the mockingbird said. "And how do we get out?"

Peggy climbed down into the pit. She shone the flashlight around the sides. "It looks as if there's a door here," she said. "But I don't think it's the same one we came through before."

"It's covered with dirt." Brian started to scrape away the dirt with his hands.

Fred leaned over the top of the pit.

"Maybe this will help." He pulled the dagger out of his belt and handed it to Brian.

At the first touch of the sharp blade, the dirt slid off the door. Brian jumped back. "Whoops! I've started a landslide." He handed the dagger back to Fred.

The pit started to fill with a cloud of dust. Peggy put her hands over her nose and mouth. She shut her eyes. When she opened them, she was standing in a pile of dirt that reached almost to the tops of her rubber boots. In front of her she saw a tall door in the side of the pit. It had a heavy iron handle and a big keyhole.

Peggy tried the handle. The door was locked. She fished the little golden key out of her pocket and put it into the keyhole. She turned the key, and the lock clicked.

Brian grabbed the handle and pulled the door open. A blast of icy air hit him in the face.

"Br-r-r!" Brian untied his jacket from around his waist and put it on.

Peggy was about to put on her jacket when she noticed Fred's tunic. "That's not very warm, Fred. Maybe you should stay here and wait for us."

Fred smiled. "I feel so happy to be my right size that nothing's going to bother me." He jumped into the pit and walked through the doorway into a narrow stone passage.

Peggy zipped up her jacket and pulled her cap over her ears. Then she and Brian stepped into the passage.

"This is not the way I came," the mockingbird said. "And I'm not at all sure I like it." He shook the dust off his feathers and fluttered onto Peggy's shoulder. "Do you mind if I don't fly in this place? I'm afraid I'll crash into something."

Puss stayed behind long enough to pile a mound of dirt against the door to keep it open. "I'm tired of keys," he said.

Fred strode along the stone passage so fast that Brian and Peggy had to run to keep up with him. Peggy beamed the flashlight ahead of them. It was very cold here.

The children were out of breath by the time they came to an iron door. It was locked. Peggy opened it with her key.

She stepped out into a shadowy place under an arch. Fred and Brian and the cat came after her. Peggy could see the shimmer of moonlight on water through the arch. She had the feeling that she'd been here before. Suddenly she knew where they were. "We're under the bridge in the park."

The mockingbird was just as surprised as Peggy. For a minute he stayed on her shoulder.

Brian ran over to the pile of newspapers on the ground under the bridge. The shopping bag was on top of the papers. Brian picked it up. "Where's Annie?"

"Come with me." The mockingbird flew off Peggy's shoulder and out from under the bridge.

The two children went after him. They heard a moaning sound from the edge of the lake. In the moonlight they saw Annie lying in the snow.

"Oh, Annie! What's the matter?" Peggy said.

Annie stopped moaning and looked

up. "Peggy! Brian! What are you doing here at this time of night?"

Fred stepped out into the open. "We came to help you, Annie. Are you hurt?"

"The moonlight was so beautiful on the water," Annie said, "that I came out to look at it. I fell and hurt my ankle. I can't walk."

Fred bent down and picked Annie up. "You don't weigh much more than a child." He carried her under the bridge.

Annie caught sight of Puss. "What's that cat doing here? Where's my shopping bag?"

Brian handed her the shopping bag. Annie felt inside it.

"I can't leave you here," Fred said.

"Are you the children's father?" Annie asked.

"No," Fred told her. "I'm the owner of the cat."

"He's the owner of the tablecloth, too," Brian said.

Annie clutched the shopping bag. She looked frightened.

Peggy laid her hand on Annie's arm. "We know you need the tablecloth, Annie, but Fred needs it too."

"Why don't you go to live in Fred's castle?" Brian said. "Then you could share the tablecloth."

136

Fred smiled. "How about it, Annie? It's a big place. There's plenty of room for both of us."

"It's a lovely place," Peggy told her. "And Brian and I can come to visit you there."

"Annie," Brian said, "it's warm where Fred lives."

Annie looked around at the snowy park. "Well," she said, "if you're sure it won't be too much trouble — "

Peggy walked back to the iron door. She held the flashlight so they could all see where they were going.

"If you don't mind," the mocking-bird said, "I'd rather stay here. I don't like being underground."

Fred carried Annie along the stone passage. It seemed warmer here now. And the passage was shorter. It ended quite suddenly.

There was no sign of the door Puss had propped open. Instead they came to a heavy curtain. Peggy held it to one side. Fred carried Annie into a round room with a four-poster bed in the middle. The moonlight sifted through a tall, narrow window in the thick wall.

"We're back in the castle!" Brian said.

Fred put Annie on a heavy carved chair. "Do you think you'll be all right here?"

"Yes, thank you." Annie looked around the room. "Doesn't anybody ever clean this place?"

"Come on, kids. It's time we went home." Puss started back along the stone passage. Brian and Peggy hurried after him.

"Where do you think we'll come out this time, Peg?" Brian asked.

Peggy had been wondering the same thing. It didn't take long for them to find out.

The passage led right to the door

that was propped open with a mound of dirt. They were back in the pit under the beech tree.

Peggy looked around for a sharp stone. "I guess we have to dig our way out."

"Don't be too sure. With this tree, you never know." Puss leaped to the ledge above. He pushed his nose against the little hole in the trunk. It began to stretch.

Brian climbed up a root and followed the cat through the hole.

Peggy went after him. She clicked off the flashlight and pushed through the bark to the park outside. Puss and Brian were waiting for her on the snowy walk.

"How about a lift home?" the cat said.

Peggy picked him up. She could feel the cat shivering.

"It's much too cold for you." Peggy tucked Puss under her jacket. She left the top unzipped just enough for him to peek out. "Why didn't you stay with Fred?" she asked the cat.

Puss rubbed his furry head against her chin. "I can always drop by to see how he's getting on." The cat began to purr. "Magic is all very well, Peggy. But that tablecloth never brought forth anything to compare with your mother's pot roast."

They started to walk toward the park gate. Suddenly Brian stopped. "Oh, Peg! How are we going to get back into our house? Mom and Dad will have a fit if we ring the bell."

Peggy pulled the magic key out of her pocket. It gleamed in the moonlight.

Brian looked at it. "No wonder Fred's father hid it. It's not safe to have that key lying around where just anyone can get hold of it."

"Listen!" Peggy turned around to look back at the beech tree.

The mockingbird was sitting on the top-most branch. He was singing to the moon.

The moonlight shone on the twisted lumps on the trunk of the old tree. Every lump seemed to have a face on it. And now Peggy was sure that all the little faces were laughing. Peggy felt like laughing too.

Other books by Ruth Chew available in paperback
from Scholastic